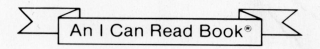

An I Can Read Book®

STAN
THE
HOT DOG
MAN

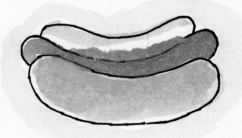

by Ethel and Leonard Kessler

HarperCollins*Publishers*

This book is a presentation of Newfield Publications, Inc.
Newfield Publications offers book clubs for children
from preschool through high school. For further
information write to: **Newfield Publications, Inc.,**
4343 Equity Drive, Columbus, Ohio 43228.

Published by arrangement with HarperCollins Publishers.
Newfield Publications is a federally registered
trademark of Newfield Publications, Inc.
I Can Read Book is a registered trademark
of HarperCollins Publishers.

Library of Congress Cataloging-in-Publication Data
Kessler, Ethel.
    Stan the hot dog man /   by Ethel and Leonard Kessler.
        p. cm. — (An I can read book)
Summary: After he retires, Stan becomes a hot dog man and finds
that his new job helps him come to the rescue during a big
snowstorm.
    ISBN 0-06-023279-X $. — ISBN 0-06-023280-3(lib. bdg.)
$
    [1. Frankfurters—Fiction. 2. Occupations. 3. Snow—Fiction.]
I. Kessler, Leonard P. , 1920- II. Title.
III. Series.
PZ7.K483St 1990   89-34474
[E]—dc20   CIP
                                                          AC

Printed in the U.S.A. All rights reserved.
2 3 4   5 6 7 8 9 10
First Edition

For Betsy, Paul, Kim,
Matt and Rick,
who love hot dogs

"Hip, hip, hooray!

Stan is sixty-five today,"

sang the bakers.

It was Stan's last day

at the bakery.

4

His friends gave him a party.

His wife, Emma, gave him

a big hug.

5

"Thank you for the watch

and the fishing rod,"

Stan said.

"Catch a big fish tomorrow,"

said his friend Jim.

"I am not ready

to stop working," said Stan.

"Tomorrow I begin

my new job."

"What is your new job?" asked Jim.

"Go to the corner of Lake Road

and Wood Lane tomorrow,

and you will see," said Stan.

"Good luck," called his friends.

The next morning

Stan woke up before it was light.

"I can sleep late today,"

he said.

"I don't work

at the bakery anymore."

Stan smiled.

He closed his eyes

and went back to sleep.

At nine o'clock the alarm rang.

"Wake up, sleepyhead!" said Emma.

Stan got dressed and ate breakfast.

He looked at his new watch.

"Time to go to work," he said.

Stan opened the garage door.

"It is the nicest hot dog truck

I ever saw," said Stan.

"Here is your cap," said Emma.

"Now you look like

a hot dog man!"

Stan climbed into the truck.

He started the engine

and drove off.

Emma waved good-bye.

It was a sunny morning.

Stan turned on the radio.

He sang with the music.

"This is more fun

than working in a hot bakery,"

he thought.

Stan parked his truck

at the corner of Lake Road

and Wood Lane.

He opened the window of the truck.

He cooked the hot dogs.

Stan waited and waited.

He looked at his watch.

"I hope people will stop here

for lunch," he thought.

A school bus stopped.

"Those hot dogs smell great,"

the driver said.

"Two dogs with mustard, please."

"You are my first customer.

Your hot dogs are free," said Stan.

"Thank you," said the bus driver.

"My name is Pat.

I drive down Lake Road every day.

I will stop here tomorrow."

Then Stan's friend Jim drove up.

"Hey, Stan! You are a hot dog man!"

shouted Jim.

"You bake the buns.

I sell the hot dogs," said Stan.

"We miss you at the bakery,"

said Jim.

"I miss you too," said Stan,

"but I like my new job.

Have a hot dog," he said.

21

Stan's first day was busy.

He sold hot dogs with relish

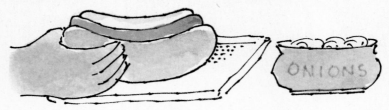

and hot dogs with onions.

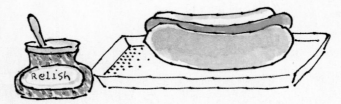

He sold hot dogs with sauerkraut

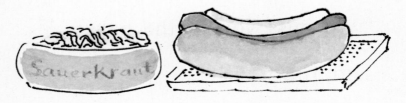

and hot dogs with mustard.

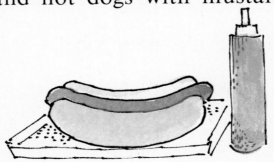

He sold the last hot dog.

"Now I can go home

and see Emma," Stan said.

Stan sang all the way home.

"How was your first day?"

asked Emma.

"Lots of people stopped for lunch,"

said Stan.

"I sold all the hot dogs.

I like being a hot dog man.

I go to work late

and come home early."

"Now we have time

to go fishing," said Emma.

"Good," said Stan.

"I will put our fishing rods

in the truck."

25

The next day

a family of four

stopped by in an old car.

"How much are your hot dogs?"
asked the mother.

"One dollar each," said Stan.

"We can only spend two dollars,"
said the father.

"Please give us two hot dogs."

"You are lucky," said Stan.

"We have a sale today.

Buy one hot dog.

Get one free!

So you can have

four hot dogs for two dollars,"

he said.

"Thank you," said the mother.

"What do you want
on your hot dogs?"
Stan asked the children.
"EVERYTHING," they yelled.
"That is how I like
my hot dogs too," said Stan.

The family waved good-bye.

"Good luck," Stan called.

Five days a week

the hot dog truck

was parked on the corner

of Lake Road and Wood Lane.

On busy days

Emma helped Stan.

She took the orders.

Stan cooked the hot dogs.

After they sold the last hot dog,
they went fishing.

"I've got one!" yelled Stan.

"I've got one too!" shouted Emma.

"What a big fish," said Stan.

"We can cook it for supper."

Some nights Stan played checkers

with Jim.

"Is the hot dog truck

ready for winter?" Jim asked.

"I put on snow tires

last week," Stan said.

"I have sand and warm blankets

in the truck."

One cold morning

Stan looked out the window.

The sky was dark and gray.

He listened to the radio

for the weather report.

"We will see light snow today,
but it will stop by noon,"
said the weather reporter.
"I think you should stay home,"
Emma said to Stan.

"I will be fine," Stan said.

"The report said

there will only be light snow."

Stan put on his warm clothes.

"Don't forget your boots,"

said Emma.

Stan parked the truck.

It started to snow.

The snow covered the road.

Soon the snow covered

the hot dog truck.

Stan turned on the radio.

"Late weather news.

Very heavy snow

with high winds today,"

said the reporter.

"No one will buy hot dogs,"

said Stan.

"I will go home."

"Stan!" called Pat.

"Did you hear the news?

This is a bad storm.

School closed early.

I must drive

Tom and Jenny home.

You should drive home too,"

she said.

"I will," said Stan.

"Follow my bus," said Pat.

Deep snow covered the highway.

The bus skidded

on the slippery road.

Pat parked her bus.

Stan parked his truck

behind the bus.

"It is not safe to drive,"

called Pat.

"Let's wait for the snowplow."

"We are cold," said Tommy.

"Come into the truck,"

said Stan.

"We will be warm there,

but first I need Jenny's help.

May I borrow your red scarf?"

he asked.

The wind blew the snow

up against the truck.

One hour went by.

They listened to the radio.

"Cars and busses

are stalled by the storm,"

said the reporter.

"That's us!" said Tommy.

"I am hungry," said Jenny.

"We have lots of hot dogs,"

said Stan.

"Please tell us a story,"

said Tommy.

"I will tell you

about the biggest fish

I ever caught,"

said Stan.

Just before dark

it stopped snowing.

A big snowplow

drove down the highway.

"There is a school bus!"

said the driver.

"We will plow the road

so it can get out."

55

"There is no one in the bus,"

said the other man.

"Where is the bus driver?

Where are the children?"

"Look! There is a red scarf.

Someone needs help!"

said the driver.

The men plowed a path

to the hot dog truck.

They opened the back door.

"I am glad you found us!
Here are the children,"
said Stan.

"We are safe and warm,

thanks to Stan," said Pat.

"We are not hungry, either,"

said Jenny.

"We cleared the road

with our snowplow,"

said the driver.

"You can drive home now."

"Hooray!" the children cheered.

"I will stop and call Emma.

Then I will drive home too,"

said Stan.

"Drive carefully,"

said the snowplow driver.

"Don't go yet!"

Stan called.

"Have a hot dog.

It is a snowstorm special."